THE  AYS OF  OYALTY

WRITTEN BY KRIS VALLOTTON
ILLUSTRATED BY MATTHEW THAYER

The Ways of Royalty
Written by Kris Vallotton
Illustrated by Matthew Thayer
Cover Concept & Design by Matthew Thayer

IBSN-978-0-9856859-6-6

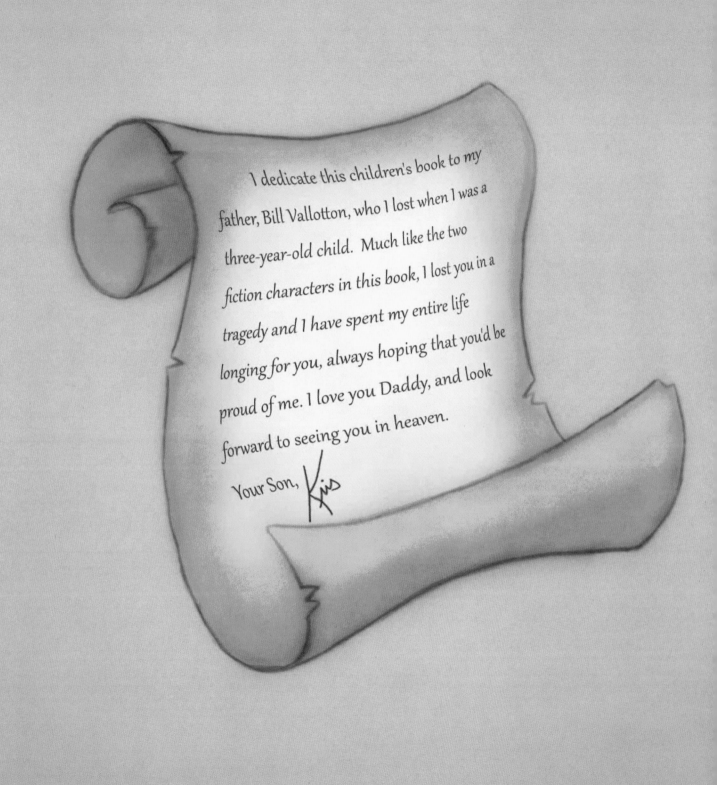

I dedicate this children's book to my father, Bill Vallotton, who I lost when I was a three-year-old child. Much like the two fiction characters in this book, I lost you in a tragedy and I have spent my entire life longing for you, always hoping that you'd be proud of me. I love you Daddy, and look forward to seeing you in heaven.

Your Son, Kris

HERE ONCE WAS A ROYAL FAMILY
THAT LIVED IN A GREAT PALACE,
THEY HAD TWO CHILDREN NAMED PETER AND ALICE.
THEY WERE HONEST, HAPPY, AND NEVER BEHAVED JEALOUS.

THEY HELPED THE TOWN'S PEOPLE WHO WERE POOR AND BROKEN, FEEDING AND CLOTHING CHILDREN WHO HAD NEVER EVEN SPOKEN.

THEN ONE DAY THERE WAS A TERRIBLE FIRE.
THEIR PARENTS WERE LOST,
THE SITUATION WAS DIRE.
THE PALACE WAS REDUCED TO ONE BIG HEAP,
AND EVERYONE WHO PASSED BY STARTED TO WEEP.

ut Alice and Peter were saved from the flames, adopted by a family that changed their last names.

GONE WAS THEIR ROYALTY AND
GOODNESS, SO SAD.
REPLACED BY PARENTS WHO TREATED THEM BAD.
THEY RAISED THEM AS PAUPERS,
DISHONEST AND MEAN,
THEY LONGED TO BE RESCUED
FROM THIS TERRIBLE SCHEME.

ETER AND ALICE FORGOT WHO THEY WERE,
SO THEY STRUGGLED WITH EVIL
THAT STARTED TO STIR.

ETER'S PAIN SOARED AS HIGH AS THE SKY...IT KEPT HIM SO ANGRY ALL HE DID WAS CRY.

ALICE BECAME NAUGHTY,
MOUTHY AND SLY,
AND DID BAD THINGS,
NEVER ASKING HERSELF WHY.

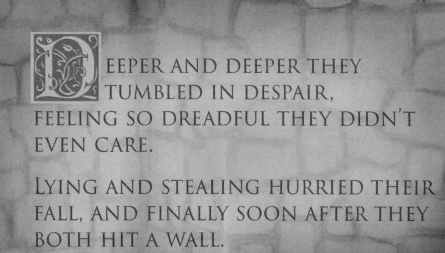

DEEPER AND DEEPER THEY
TUMBLED IN DESPAIR,
FEELING SO DREADFUL THEY DIDN'T
EVEN CARE.

LYING AND STEALING HURRIED THEIR
FALL, AND FINALLY SOON AFTER THEY
BOTH HIT A WALL.

HEN ALL SEEMED LOST THEY MET A GREAT FELLOW, WHO REACHED OUT WITH LOVE TO SAVE THEM FROM TROUBLE.

E RECOVERED TWO CROWNS FROM THE PALACE'S RUBBLE, AND SEARCHED FOR TWO PEOPLE WHO WERE HUMBLE AND NOBLE.

PETER AND ALICE
BOWED AT HIS FEET
AS HE ROBED THEM
WITH RIGHTEOUSNESS
AND
CROWNED THEM
WITH PEACE.

SUDDENLY PETER SHOUTED WITH JOY, "I REMEMBER WHO I AM, I AM NOT A BAD BOY. BORN TO A KING WHO WAS PURE AND RIGHT...NOW IT'S MY TURN TO LOVE AND NOT FIGHT. ALL THE WHILE I HAD THE WRONG NAME. I FORGOT WHO I WAS, AND I WASN'T THE SAME."

 LICE PUT ON HER BEAUTIFUL CROWN, AND HEARD FROM HEAVEN A VERY GREAT SOUND. SUDDENLY HER HEART AND SOUL TURNED AROUND, AND FROM THAT DAY ON SHE WAS AS HAPPY AS A CLOWN.

RIENDS CAME TO REBUILD
THE GREAT CASTLE,
STONE UPON STONE,
THEY LAID WITH NO HASSLE.
JOYFULLY THEY HUNG ITS DOORS
AND ITS GATES, LAUGHING AS THEY
WORKED, NOBODY WAS LATE.

BUT THAT'S NOT THE END OF
THEIR WONDERFUL STORY;
THEY WENT ON TO RESTORE ROYALTY AND GLORY.
AN EXCITING KINGDOM ROSE IN THE NIGHT,
AND THOUSANDS CAME TO SEE
THE VERY GREAT SIGHT.

ETER AND ALICE WERE CHEERFUL AND GLAD, AS THEY WATCHED MANY PEOPLE LEARN THEY'RE NOT BAD. SO MANY CHILDREN LOST THEIR SAD FROWNS, REPLACED FOREVER WITH BEAUTIFUL CROWNS!

So wherever you are
the Kingdom is near;
you see, it's within you,
there is nothing to fear!

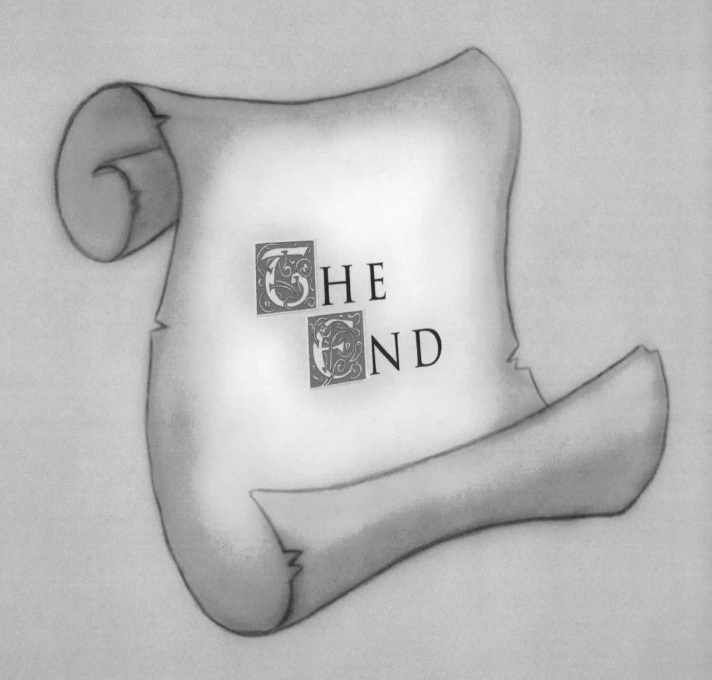

KRIS VALLOTTON
AUTHOR

Kris is the senior associate leader at Bethel Church in Redding, California; the cofounder and senior overseer of the Bethel School of Supernatural Ministry; and the founder of Moral Revolution. He has written several bestselling books, including *Heavy Rain* and *The Supernatural Ways of Royalty*, and is a much-sought-after international speaker, where his personal testimony of deliverance brings hope and freedom to thousands.

MATTHEW THAYER
ILLUSTRATOR

Matthew and his wife, Joy, live in Redding, California with their children. He has been drawing cartoons since he was two years old and is the illustrator of several books, including the "Loving On Purpose" children's series. Matthew is also an award winning filmmaker, a graphic design artist, and the co-founder of speropictures. www.speropictures.com

Other Books by
Kris Vallotton

The Supernatural Ways of Royalty

Developing a Supernatural Lifestyle

Moral Revolution

How Heaven Invades Earth

Spirit Wars

Outrageous Courage

The Supernatural Power of Forgiveness

Basic Training for the Prophetic Ministry

Basic Training for the Supernatural Ways of Royalty

Fashioned to Reign

KV MINISTRIES
www.kvministries.com

KV Ministries

www.kvministries.com